AGON
DOGNAPPERS
FINALLY
DRAGON SIGHT
GEORGIE WINS
GARDENING
PRIZE AGAIN
COUPON
GET YOUR FREE
DRAGON PLANT
SEEDS
BIG CAT BACK?

For the little seed I am growing...

First published in Great Britain in 2021 by Pavilion Children's Books
This edition published in Great Britain in 2023 by Farshore
An imprint of HarperCollins*Publishers*
1 London Bridge Street, London SE1 9GF
www.farshore.co.uk

HarperCollins*Publishers*
Macken House, 39/40 Mayor Street Upper
Dublin 1, D01 C9W8

Text and illustrations copyright © Emma Lazell 2021
Emma Lazell has asserted her moral rights.

ISBN 978 1 8436 5488 9
Printed in Great Britain by Bell and Bain Ltd, Glasgow.
002

A CIP catalogue record for this title is available from the British Library.

Stay safe online. Any website addresses listed in this book are correct at
the time of going to print. However, Farshore is not responsible for content
hosted by third parties. Please be aware that online content can be subject
to change and websites can contain content that is unsuitable for children.
We advise that all children are supervised when using the internet.

Farshore takes its responsibility to the planet and its inhabitants very
seriously. We aim to use papers from well-managed forests run by
responsible suppliers.

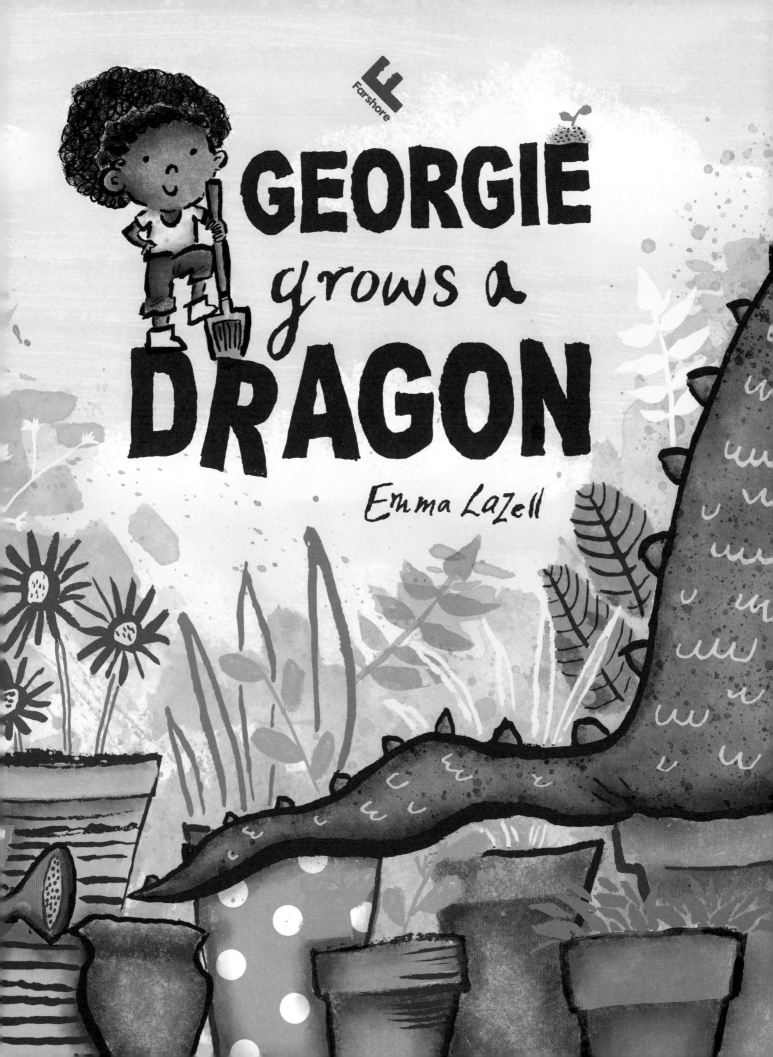

GEORGIE grows a DRAGON

Emma Lazell

Farshore

Georgie was a little girl who loved
to grow flowers and plants.
Each night, before bed, she thought
about what to grow next.

But one night... as she slept...

plop!

"Oh
wow!
I've
grown a
dragon!"

Georgie had never grown a **dragon** before.

In fact she didn't even remember planting one.

And the dragon
was nothing like
her other plants.

It was
bigger,

hungrier

and
much more
troublesome!

This plant didn't want to be put in the sun.

It didn't like its new soil,

and it didn't even want to be watered!

he he he

EXTRA STINKY COMPOST

Bash!

Smash!

The dragon didn't make
a very good house plant.

It didn't even fit in the greenhouse.

And the other plants made it…

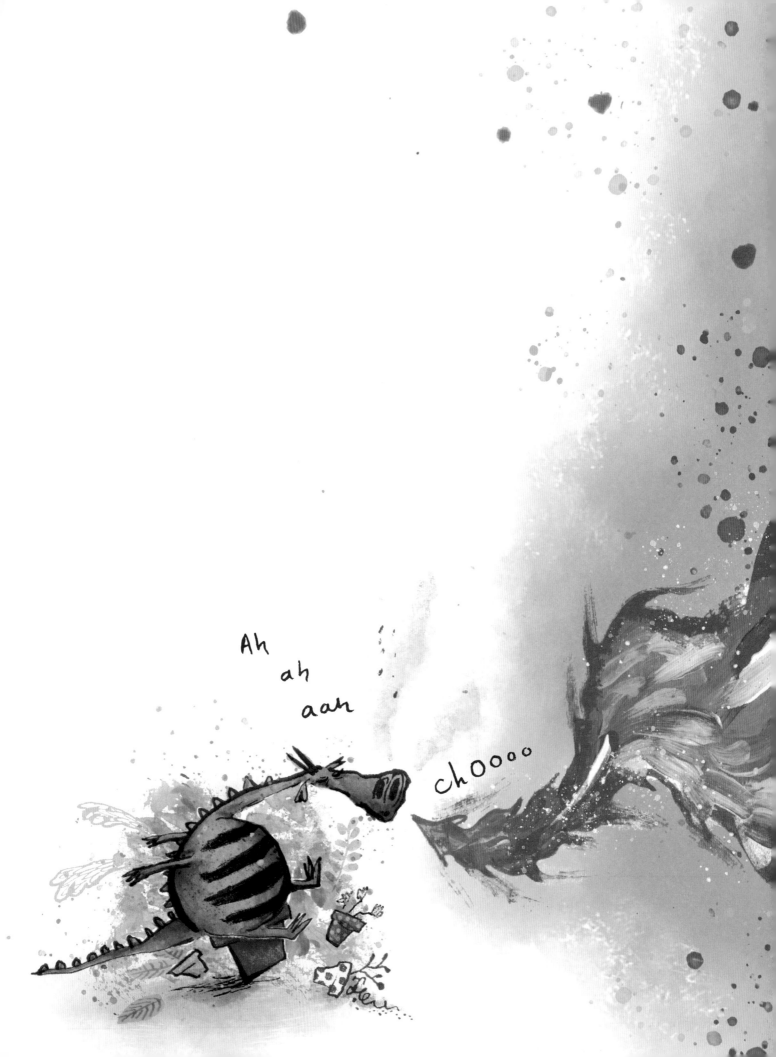

"Oh
Dragon...

...**why** are you so difficult?

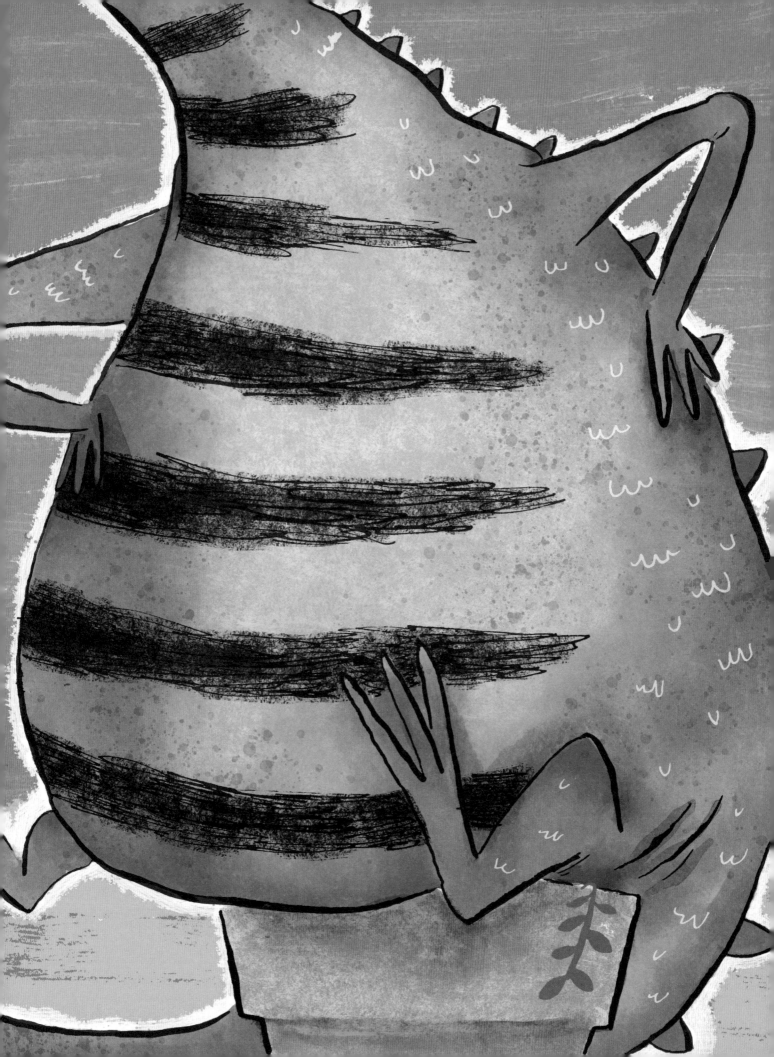

"I'll tell you why!
It's becasue I've got
a great big
pot

stuck
on
my
bot,

and I am
most definitely

not

not

not
a plant," he huffed.

Once Dragon
was unpotted

he was
much less
trouble.

In fact, he was
extremely
friendly,

very kind,

incredibly
practical...

...and super-helpful
when Georgie was
late for school!

But now that Dragon had
popped out of his pot…

...he was keen to fly off
to his family again.

Both were sad to say goodbye,
but they knew they'd
always be friends.

And anyway…

... Georgie seemed to have grown **another** new plant!